P9-CDL-738

YOUNG LARRY

Daniel Pinkwater

Illustrated by
Jill Pinkwater

MARSHALL CAVENDISH • NEW YORK

LARRY

lived on the shore of Baffin Bay with his mother, and his brother, Roy. Their father was a big bear, who had once eaten a whale.

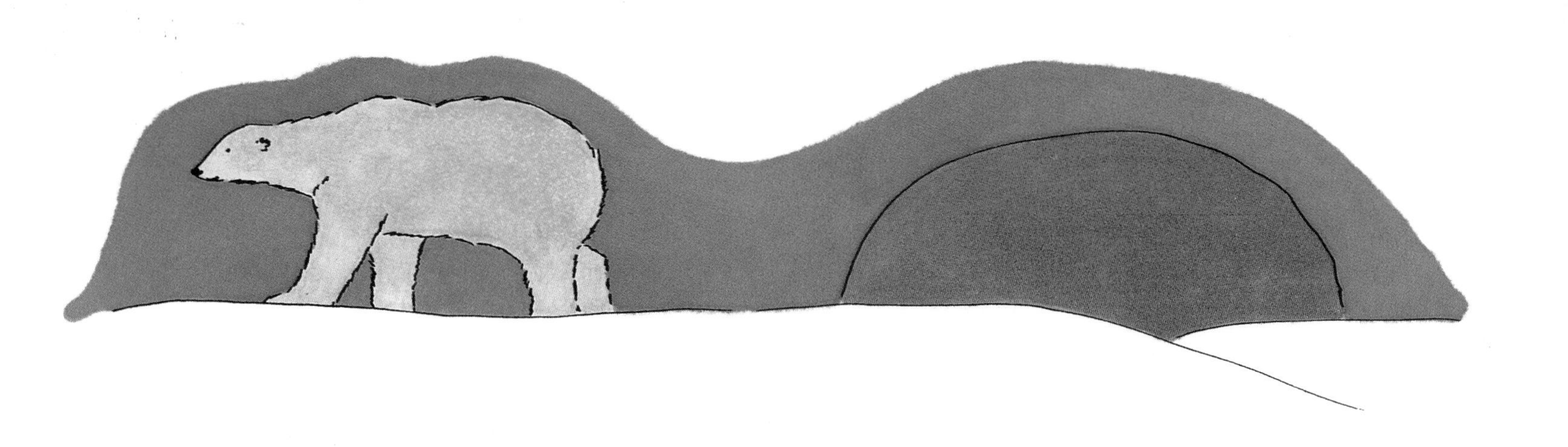

Once or twice, Larry and Roy had seen their father a long way off.

"That bear is your father," their mother told them. "He found a dead whale one time, and ate the whole thing himself."

Larry and Roy were proud of their father.

"Some day, when we are big polar bears, maybe we can hunt with our father," Larry said.

"I doubt it," their mother said. "He would probably give you a hit in the head, and tell you to get lost."

"Why would he do that to his own cubs?" Larry asked.

"Polar bear fathers are like that," their mother said.

"It doesn't seem very nice," Larry said.

"One day, I will give you a hit in the head myself," their mother said. "And send you off to take care of yourselves."

"Wow. That is harsh," Larry and Roy said.

"It is Nature's way," Larry and Roy's mother said.

"Well, I don't like it," Larry said.

"Nobody is asking you to like it. You are bears. Get used to it."

Being hit in the head and sent to take care of themselves was a long way off. They had plenty of time to play, and swim, and follow their mother around, and learn to hunt, and swallow little fishes.

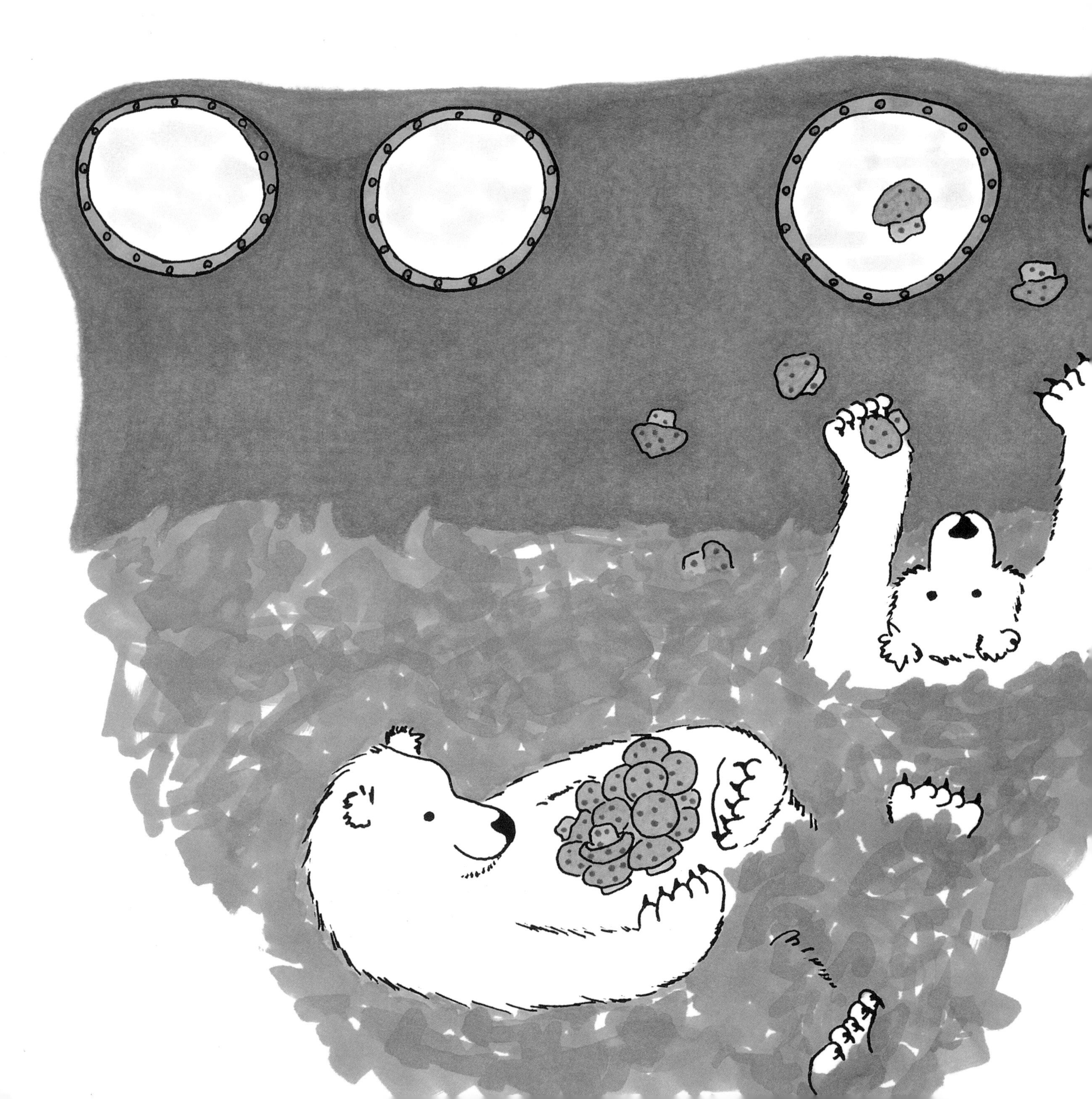

Once a boat came. It was full of humans. Larry and Roy swam out to look at them.

The humans took pictures of Larry and Roy. They seemed happy to see them. They threw blueberry muffins to them, and Larry and Roy ate them. After a while, the humans stopped throwing blueberry muffins, and Larry and Roy swam away to find their mother.

“What were those animals in that . . . thing?” Larry asked his mother.

“Those are humans,” Larry and Roy’s mother said. It is OK to eat them, but they taste funny.”

“Maybe I will eat one some time,” Roy said.

“I would rather eat those things with the blueberries,” Larry said.

The day finally came when Larry and Roy's mother called them to her, and hit each of them in the head.

"Get lost," she said. "Go and fend for yourselves."

Then she went away to see what Larry and Roy's father was doing.

"So, do you think we know how to fend?" Larry asked Roy.

"More or less," Roy said.

Larry and Roy found they were able to take care of themselves. They were medium-sized polar bears by this time, and each was nine-and-a-half feet tall, when standing on his hind legs.

Roy liked being a grown-up bear more than Larry did. Larry thought it was boring to spend all his time looking for things to eat.

Sometimes he dreamed about the time the humans had come in the boat, and how much he had liked the blueberry muffins. It was the only thing ever to happen to him that did not happen every day.

"I am going to take a nap for a week or two," Larry said. "I will go to sleep right here, on this chunk of ice."

"I am going to look for something to hit on the head and eat," Roy said. "After that, I might take a nap myself."

Larry curled up on the ice, and went to sleep. Even though it was nearly summer, it began to snow. The snow fell, and fell heavier.

Soon he was covered with snow. It was warm under the snow. He slept deeply, breathing slow.

He never heard the crunching sound, when the chunk of ice he was sleeping on, broke loose from the shore, and floated out into the middle of Baffin Bay.

Larry dreamed about the things he knew—swimming in icy water, protected by his thick fur—playing with Roy when they were cubs—his mother—and the far-off sight of his father, who had eaten a whale—and the time the humans had given him blueberry muffins.

Larry's ice chunk floated to the south, farther and farther.

FISH CAKES • MU
CINE

As Larry floated to the south, the water got warmer, and his ice chunk began to melt.

It got smaller and smaller. Larry kept sleeping.

By the time Larry reached the waters off Bayonne, New Jersey, the ice-chunk wasn't much bigger than he was. He slid off the ice, and into the water.

Then he woke up.

Larry swam for the shore. When he came out of the water, the first thing he saw was a human. The human was eating a muffin.

"Does that have blueberries?" Larry asked the human.

"No, it has banana," the human said. "You may have it."

The human put the banana muffin down on the beach, and ran away.

Larry ate the banana muffin.

"This is as good as those other ones," he thought.

"Hey, human!" Larry shouted. "How do I get more of these?"

The human was still running away. He shouted over his shoulder. "You get a job, and they give you money! Then you exchange money for muffins!"

"It seems perfectly simple," Larry thought. "I wonder what a job is."

Larry wandered along the beach, until he met another human.

"Hello, human," Larry said. "Where can I find a job?"

"What can you do? What are you good at?" the human asked.

"I can swim," Larry said.

"Do you want to be a lifeguard?" the human asked.

"Yes. I do. What is a lifeguard?" Larry asked.

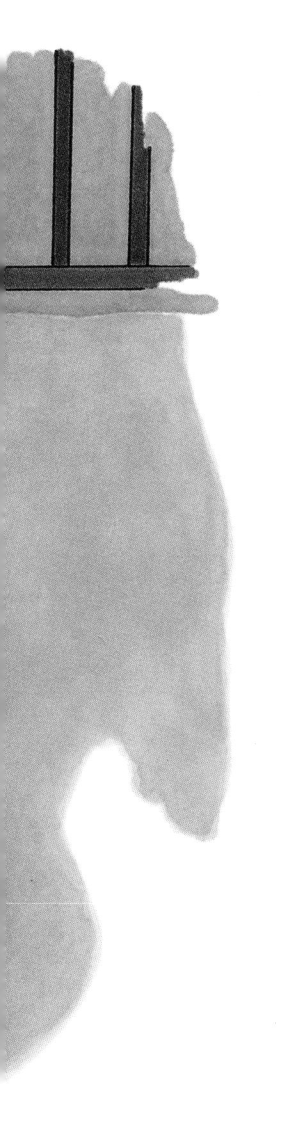

A lifeguard is someone who sits on a high tower, and looks out for people who are drowning. When the lifeguard sees one, he swims out and saves that person's life.

Larry became a lifeguard. Every week, the Chief Life-guard gave him money, and Larry would exchange the money for muffins, mostly blueberry, but also banana.

"This is much better than life at home," Larry thought.

One day, the Chief Lifeguard told Larry, "It has been brought to my attention that you are a polar bear."

"I have never claimed to be anything else," Larry said.

"Well, after today, you may no longer be a lifeguard."

"Why is that?" Larry asked.

"It is because, as I have been informed, polar bears eat people."

"This is true, but I have never done so," Larry said. "I prefer to eat muffins, blueberry, and sometimes banana. Besides, I was told that humans taste funny."

"All the same," the Chief Lifeguard said, "I will not take the risk."

This might have been a sad day for Larry, if a Mr. Martin Frobisher had not gone out in a little row-boat, to get healthful exercise.

Mr. Frobisher's boat went upside-down, Larry saw it happen, and swam out to rescue him.

"Be calm, sir," Larry said. "Your life is saved."

"Glub-glub," said Mr. Frobisher.

When they were both ashore, Mr. Frobisher said, "You have saved my life. I wish to give you a reward."

"Oh, you need not do that," Larry said.

"But I insist," Mr. Frobisher said. "Tell what you most desire."

"After today, I will no longer be a life-guard," Larry said. "I will have no way to pay for the muffins I dearly love."

"I am a rich man!" Mr. Frobisher said. "I will buy a fine hotel, with a swimming pool. You may be the lifeguard there!"

"And you will pay me each week in money or muffins?" Larry asked.

"Of course!" Mr. Frobisher said.

"Will you promise never to hit me in the head and tell me to go away and look after myself?" Larry asked.

"Never, unless you should eat a guest, or any other person," Mr. Frobisher said.

"I have never so much as tasted a human," Larry said.

"In that case," Mr. Frobisher said. "You have a job and a home for life!"

Mr. Frobisher and Larry went off, hand-in-paw, to find a bakery, and a big bag of muffins.

To each other,

D. P. and J. P.

Marshall Cavendish, 99 White Plains Road, Tarrytown, New York 10591
The text of this book is set in 16 point Esprit Book
The illustrations are rendered in pen and ink and colored markers
Printed in Italy
First edition
3 5 6 4 2

Library of Congress Cataloging-in-Publication Data. Pinkwater, Daniel Manus date.
Young Larry / Daniel Pinkwater ; illustrated by Jill Pinkwater. p. cm. Summary: After being hit on the head by his mother and told to fend for himself, Larry the polar bear floats from Baffin Bay to New Jersey where he gets a job as a lifeguard. ISBN 0-7614-5004-1 (reinforced bdg.)
[1. Polar bear—Fiction. 2. Bears—Fiction. 3. Humorous stories.] I. Pinkwater, Jill, ill. II. Title.
PZ7.P6335Yp 1998 [E]—dc20 96-41670 CIP AC